A VERY URGENT MATTER

CONNOR WHITELEY

No part of this book may be reproduced in any form or by any electronic or mechanical means. Including information storage, and retrieval systems, without written permission from the author except for the use of brief quotations in a book review.

This book is NOT legal, professional, medical, financial or any type of official advice.

Any questions about the book, rights licensing, or to contact the author, please email connorwhiteley@connorwhiteley.net

Copyright © 2023 CONNOR WHITELEY

All rights reserved.

DEDICATION
Thank you to all my readers without you I couldn't do what I love.

CHAPTER 1
1st May 2022
Canterbury, England

Private Eye Bettie English loved May in Canterbury. There was just something so special about the month with all the university students coming back from their Easter break and the wonderfully warm spring air created such a wonderful atmosphere.

For the past month Canterbury had seemed strange without so many amazing university students with their talking, laughing and partying that always happened on the high street where Bettie's office was. And finally the student life was starting to return to the city so finally it started to feel alive once more, and the utterly wonderful spring weather only reinforced that feeling.

Bettie continued to stare out of her large office window and down onto the cobblestone high street where she could hear the students happy to see each other once again, catching up about their break and even some of the local musicians were out playing on the amazingly warm spring day.

But the thing that Bettie truly loved about May was every single breathtakingly good bakery was opening back up filling the air with the utterly sensational smells of their freshly baked bread that melted into buttery deliciousness, sweet creamy cakes and some had their rich meaty pastries too on offer.

Sadly because Bettie was pregnant and her body didn't like it, she wouldn't stand at the window for too long with all those sensational smells. Otherwise her body would want to vomit at all the animal products, but Bettie just wanted to admire the spring May day for a little longer.

And she really wanted any excuse not to return to her laptop and continue doing those backgrounds checks that one of her contract businesses had given her to do.

Bettie only had a few left but after doing twenty this morning, Bettie wasn't sure if she wanted to do much more.

At this point she would almost give anything to have a break or something else to do. But the background check contracts paid well and most often than not they were fascinating.

Sometimes Bettie felt like the only reason why she became a Private Eye was so she could dig into people's lives and get paid for it. It was amazing what some people got up to in their youth, spare time and just for fun.

"Auntie!" a young man shouted.

Bettie smiled as she focused on the high street once more and saw her wonderful nephew Sean waving at her and he started to make his way up to her office. Bettie supposed she should have unlocked the door for him, but Bettie wanted to feel the warming sun on her skin for a couple more moments.

Bettie knew it was strange to love the sun, warmth and seeing young university students again. But after the absolutely awful weather with storms, rain and even some threat to life warnings, Bettie was more than glad to see some sun again.

She was even more happy to see her nephew who went away with his boyfriend to Glasgow for two weeks last month. Bettie hadn't seen him for ages and she really, really wanted to catch up.

The sound of her laptop beeping made Bettie frown as she realised that she was getting more and more emails. Bettie knew it was the same sender and in the past ten minutes alone they had been sending her an email a minute.

Bettie wouldn't have minded too much if they were about different things, but each email was the same.

It was from an insurance company.

Now Bettie had no problems with UK insurance companies because it turned out they had a lot of money, a lot of business and most importantly they weren't that evil. So Bettie liked them.

But this particular insurance company was offering her £50,000 to help them with "a matter most secretive and urgent".

To Bettie that meant one of two things. It was either extremely complex both personally and legally and they couldn't get the cops involved. Or it meant it was just plain illegal.

And Bettie did not want to get involved in illegal business or shenanigans. She didn't want to give birth to a baby in prison, that was not her idea of fun.

The laptop beeped again.

Sean knocked on the door, Bettie went over and opened it to him. Then she went to her large wooden desk and sat down, gesturing to Sean to sit down on one of the two chairs in front of the desk.

"Hi Auntie," Sean said, grinning.

Bettie partly didn't want to know why Sean was grinning, but she couldn't deny it was great seeing him. He was wearing his normal outfit which was nothing more than some skinny jeans, a t-shirt and his longish blond hair with some pink streaks styled through it.

Bettie was still impressed Sean managed to pull it off. He was probably the only person she had ever met who could.

"Graham told me the news. You're expecting twins!" Sean said.

Bettie gave him a thin smile. That was what she got from agreeing last month to have the baby scan. She and her boyfriend Graham had simply wanted to find out the baby's sex, but oh no the doctor just had to reveal a bit more.

She was having twins!

One boy. One girl.

Bettie still didn't know how to feel about it. both Bettie and Graham were both still shocked it and they hadn't really spoken about it too much. Bettie... was pleased because she got the best of both worlds, but she was terrified.

Raising one child was hard enough, but two!

"You're not pleased?" Sean asked.

Bettie shrugged. "I... I don't know. I hate to do this but... can we talk about something else,"

Sean came round the desk and gave Bettie a big hug.

"Sure thing Auntie," he said.

Bettie forced down her tears. He was the first person in the entire family who had allowed her to do that, besides Graham. Everyone else had pressured her into talking about revealing how she felt, but that was where the problem lay.

Because she was so busy with seeing family (and them forcing her to talk about it) and then she had so much investigating to do. Bettie had no time to think about how she felt, in all honesty she just wanted some breathing room.

"Thank you beaut," Bettie said.

Her laptop beeped again.

"For crying out loud," Bettie said sharply.

"I only hugged you," Sean said.

"Not you. This bloody insurance company," Bettie said.

She opened the email and smiled as the insurance company had now sent her a brand new contract with a rather amazing bonus for this "most urgent case". They were now offering her all expenses paid, £100,000 fee and a free holiday.

Bettie smiled. What this insurance company wanted, they were willing to pay for it and they were clearly desperate.

There was even an address included in Dover for a place to meet them.

Bettie folded her arms. She did say she wanted a distraction and now she was going to get it.

"Sorry to cut this short Sean. I did to go," Bettie said, getting up and grabbing her things.

"Can I come please? I can drive you. Please Auntie," Sean said.

Bettie cocked her head. "Isn't this university exam season? And you are in your final year, aren't you?"

Sean smiled. "Most of my units are coursework. I have three exams in June and that's it. I'm all caught up. Please,"

Bettie rolled her eyes. It was becoming harder to drive with the bab*ies* getting larger, so as much as Bettie knew her sister was going to throw a hiss fit. She nodded.

"Come on then," Bettie said.

"Great!"

Sean rushed out the office and Bettie closed the door behind her.

Seems like she was going to Dover as fast as she could.

CHAPTER 2
1st May 2022
Dover, England

Detective Graham Adams never liked Dover for relaxing or anything else, because so much crime happened here. Of course, lots of people didn't know about all the smuggling, human trafficking and drugs related things that happened in the large Dover City, but Graham was actually happy about that.

But his job definitely spoiled his view, opinion and attitude of Dover.

The only remotely good thing about Dover had to be the massive castle with the tunnels from World War 2 under it that always looked imposing, scary and intimating as a ferry sailed through the English Channel.

Considering the amazing history of the castle, Graham was more than glad the castle had been built and was still around to this day.

He would definitely bring the twins here in the

future.

Graham forced himself not to focus on the idea of twins, so he turned his attention back to what he did best.

His job.

As Graham stood on the hard metal floor of one of the massive ferries that always came in and out of Dover tens of times a day. Graham was surprised by the sheer scale of the ship, it was easily a kilometre long and probably half that wide. Even now Graham looked like a tiny spot on the deck with hundreds of other people cramped around him.

The smell of the salty sea air, the sweaty people and the salty crisps that the ferry served filled the air, and left a horrible taste in his mouth.

But he was here for work after all.

As a Floater Detective in the Kent Police Force, Graham wasn't tied to any one department or type of crime so he simply went to whatever department he liked and was willing to have him.

And thankfully after him and his sexy girlfriend Bettie had managed to stop a major threat to National Security last month, lots more departments seemed to want his expertise.

Graham wasn't sure if he would call it expertise, but he did love his job. That was for sure.

Most recently, Border Force had reached out to Kent Police and requested Graham helped them with a police operation in France to stop drugs coming into the UK.

Of course Graham jumped at the chance to help the French, because despite all the government propaganda that made the French out to be evil, scheming idiots. They were actually some of the nicest people Graham had ever met, and they really had a great Police Force.

Needless to say Graham absolutely loved working with them.

So when he got over to France last week (without telling Bettie. He was impressed with himself) he had been told there was a British gang of drug dealing who were shipping drugs from France into Dover and then the drugs spread up to London.

Graham was hoping the drug suppliers were on the ship today, and hopefully it wouldn't be too hard to find them and stop them.

The French had told Graham to see out for someone called Stanley Ratliff. From the surveillance photos they had sent him before the ferry left, he was a little short man wearing jeans, a white shirt and carrying a very large suitcase that the drug dogs didn't detect.

That was strange. Not unheard of.

Graham knew that criminals were getting smarter and smarter to avoid getting caught by the dogs. Maybe this Stanley man had learnt or even invested in a new technique.

As a massive gust of icy wind blew past, Graham frowned and felt a number of English people smash into him and then get annoyed at him. Because clearly

Graham had forced the ferry to move and knock them over.

Some people!

Then after a few young English men swore at him, Graham shook his head and started to glide through the crowd on the ferry.

The wind kept blowing, the ship kept moving and some people were clearly suffering from sea sickness.

Then tens of metres away as the ferry rolled into a large wave, Graham saw a short little man in jeans, a white dress shirt and holding something.

Graham couldn't be sure it was Stanley unless he got closer.

Then the ship rolled again and out of the corner of his eye he saw another massive suitcase being held by a man in jeans. Again Graham couldn't be sure who to check.

Graham felt someone smash into him.

Knocking him forward.

A number of other people fell over.

Graham pushed himself up.

He expected someone to apologise to him but no, all Graham saw was a man walking on like Graham hadn't even been there.

All around Graham people were moaning, talking and pointing to the man who had presumably knocked over other people.

Then Graham realised that the man who had knocked him over was wearing skinny jeans, a red dress shirt and carrying a very large bag. But there were wheels on the bottom.

Graham laughed that was clever.

He started to follow the guy and Graham had to admit it was clever changing the t-shirt and using a 2-in-1 suitcase that could be carried and wheeled along. If the guy hadn't smashed into him, he might never caught him before the ferry docked.

Graham kept following him.

Then a young woman stepped out in front of the man and pointed to Graham.

"Excuse me. There's a strange man following you,"

Damn it!

Stanley looked at Graham.

He ran.

Throwing down his suitcase.

Graham ran after him.

People dived out the way.

There was a staircase ahead.

The ship was massive.

Graham couldn't let him escape down there.

Graham took out an apple he bought.

He threw it.

Whacking Stanley on the head.

He left.

Down the stairs.

Landing with a thud.

When Graham made his way over to the staircase, he saw that Stanley was completely unconscious and there was even blood on the staircase with even more pooling around his head.

Graham really hoped he didn't just kill someone.

"What is the meaning of this Detective Adams?" a tall woman shouted in a French accent.

Graham had no idea a French police officer was also on board. But Graham smiled when he noticed she had secured the suitcase full of drugs, and Graham realised that she was the same woman who alerted Stanley that he was following him.

"Teamwork Detective," the woman said. "Britain get the criminal. France gets the drugs,"

Graham smiled. That really was the best way to do things, at least that way everyone won and got their criminal.

Graham's phone buzzed.

It was a text from Bettie saying that her and Sean was heading to Dover if he wanted to see her, not that she was expecting it.

Graham realised he had made a mistake, and he really had to correct it.

Graham looked down at the bleeding, injured Stanley. He had to get him to a hospital then thankfully he was heading into Dover now.

He just hoped he could fix his massive mistake.

CHAPTER 3
1ˢᵗ May 2022
Dover, England

Bettie had completely forgotten how awful the drive down to Dover was with all the tourists, lorries and trucks that constantly drove in and out of the busy city. And all that bad was before Bettie remembered how English people couldn't drive.

Bettie was extremely grateful that she had Sean with her.

As Bettie stood in a large conference room that was wonderfully air-conditioned with tea, coffee and water on the table for everyone to help themselves. Bettie was starting to wonder how many people were coming in the conference room to meet them, but apparently the executives of the company were finishing a major presentation to some investors.

Bettie wanted to point out that the same executives still found the time to keep emailing her once every minute until she got here. But Bettie didn't want to be rude so early in the morning.

To Bettie's surprise though, the executives had listened to her comment about she couldn't be in the same room as cow, sheep or any other animal milk. And Bettie had never seen so many still cartons of non-animal milk. She had no idea that oat, rice and other types of milk even existed.

Bettie had only heard of coconut and soya before now.

In all honesty Bettie had just asked for that to see how desperate the insurance company was for her, and given to the lengths they were going to impress her. Bettie was starting to get extremely concerned about what they wanted her to do or investigate.

The soft, almost inaudible soothing music playing in the room only added to Bettie's unease. Clearly the company wanted Bettie and her babies to be nice and relaxed, but it was having the opposite effect in reality.

At least the company didn't have any strange smelling candles burning or whatever the gurus said was great for pregnant women these days.

Instead all Bettie could smell was the wonderful Dover sea taste that made the taste of fish and chips form on her mouth. Bettie huffed at the taste of the fish and she forced herself to forget about that.

"Is Grahs coming?" Sean asked as he sat at the conference table flicking through holiday photos.

Bettie had to admit him and his boyfriend Harry made an adorable couple and it was clear from the beautiful photos (and the silly ones) that they both ready loved each other, but Bettie didn't like the question.

She had blanked Graham from her mind for most of the week, Bettie understood that he was scared about having twins. She was too, but after the first week of finding out and having to deal with family and everything. Bettie really, really understood why he was scared.

But Bettie didn't feel the need to run off to France.

And that was what Bettie was furious about, ever since they had gotten together two-ish years ago. They had been a team, partners and they always told each other everything. But he had broken that this time.

Graham hadn't told her how he was feeling, so he ran away.

As much as Bettie didn't want to think about it, she couldn't help the tight knot in her stomach that made her question if he would run away forever when the children were born.

She knew it wasn't true, but she was still nervous.

Then she felt Sean hug her and she kissed him on the head. That was what she liked about him, he was always such a nice boy. Kind, helpful and always knew what to do in times of crisis.

And in all honesty, that was what Bettie liked about gay people. In her experience, they were always kinder, better and a lot more respectable than other men.

"I'm don't know," Bettie said. "I hope so. But we'll see,"

With a little bit of noise coming from outside the conference room, Bettie gestured Sean to sit back down and they both sat at one end of the conference table.

Then three people in black suits walked in with folders and computers and God knows what else. It was two women and one man. None of them were too old, they were probably a few years older than Bettie in their late thirties.

None of them looked happy. They all looked concerned, worried and very stressed.

"Miss English," the woman at the head of the table said calmly. "I am Mrs Madeline Fisher,"

Bettie nodded her head slightly. "I am Bettie and this is my nephew Sean,"

The other woman and man who sat either side of Madeline looked worried.

"Please know. My nephew is very good at keeping secrets, helping me on cases and I promise you he is no threat here,"

Everyone looked slightly relieved.

"I am Hunter Lewis," the man said, "and this is my wife Eva,"

Bettie nodded her respects to both of them.

"I assume you would like to know why…" Madeline trailed off.

"Have been so demanding and accommodating

to get me here," Bettie said.

Both the Lewis-es laughed a little.

Madeline opened up a folder. "Yes. I suppose you could say that Miss English. I am afraid we have a very urgent matter for you to attend to,"

"And you will honour the terms and pay you said in your email," Bettie said.

As the three of them nodded, Bettie wasn't sure if their necks were going to snap. They were nodding so ferociously.

"Believe in me Miss English, we will probably give you shares in the company at the end of this," Madeline said.

Bettie liked the sound of that.

"In case you have guessed," Hunter said, "the three of us make up the board of directors of Fisher Insurance,"

Bettie nodded. That made sense.

"Two days ago we heard from Kent Police that they were officially closing the investigation into a theft from one of our clients," Madeline said.

Bettie leant closer.

Eva nodded. "That was bad enough. But the real problem is the insurance pay out would be crippling to us,"

"How?" Sean asked. "I thought insurance companies had millions,"

Bettie smiled. That was a very good point.

"That is normally true. But we need to increase our prices and because of our stupid government accounting rules, it is far easier to do that at the end of our financial year. Which is the end of the month,"

"So Madeline," Bettie said, "you're asking me to investigate something so your business can survive for another financial year,"

Madeline nodded fiercely again. "Yes Bettie. The company will go under for sure if we have to pay out this insurance policy. But thankfully that is where you come in,"

Bettie smiled, that was going to be interesting.

Hunter Lewis opened up this folder and held up some documents.

"We have managed to convince," he said, "our client that if the stolen property is found and returned to him. Then the company does not have to pay out the claim,"

"And because the police have dropped the investigation. I am your last hope," Bettie said.

Madeline stood up. "Miss English I am begging you. Please take the case. Please help us. So many livelihoods are at stake,"

Bettie looked at Sean who was smiling at her. He knew she was going to take the case, and that was probably the only downside of having such a good relationship with him. He knew her far, far too well.

"Fine," Bettie said. "I'll take the case. Just tell me, what are stolen?"

Madeline frowned. "A million pounds worth of Macs and other laptops,"

Now the hundred thousand pound fee made

perfect sense.

CHAPTER 4
1st May 2022
Dover, England

Graham didn't know why Bettie wanted to meet in a cold abandoned multi-storey car park with no other cars nearby and the sound of dripping water echoing off the concrete walls, but Graham could only come to one single conclusion.

She wanted to kill him.

So he was sitting safely inside his black rental car with the large windows closed and Graham was constantly on the lookout for danger.

Of course, Graham knew that was ridiculous and that was never going to happen, but just in case, Graham had made sure to stop off at a local supermarket and buy her two bars of her favourite vegan chocolate. One bar was peanut butter flavoured which Graham hated with a passion, since Bettie didn't like peanut butter normally, but she loved it in chocolate.

Graham was the opposite.

Then the other bar was salted caramel, Graham really hoped she was going to share it with him. Graham loved the salty creamy flavour of the caramel, it was one of the best sweets in the entire world.

But Graham understood why Bettie was furious at him, he had abandoned her when she needed him. He had stupidly thought she was okay, but what if she wasn't?

What if the love of his life needed him?

It was completely stupid, selfish and a betrayal of her trust for Graham to do that, and he just had to make it up to her. So whatever she needed Graham was going to make sure he helped her.

The sound of another car slowly pulling up behind his rental made Graham smile when he saw it was Bettie.

Graham got out of the car and his heart skipped a couple of wonderful beats as he saw his sexy beautiful Bettie with her long brown hair, jeans and her killer smile.

Graham was expecting her to hug him or something, but instead she simply gestured him to follow her and then Graham heard the hissing of the boot of the car opening.

Now he was certain Bettie was going to kill him.

When he got to the back of the car, Graham blew a kiss at Bettie who was simply sitting on the edge of the boot with her little legs dangling as they struggled to reach the floor.

Graham sat down next to her.

"Hi Sean," Graham said as he saw him in the driver's seat and then Graham realised he was sitting on something.

He moved his bum slightly and realised it was a used condom. Graham didn't even want to know how it ended up there, but given how much Bettie was smiling she had probably found it somewhere else and put it there.

Graham smiled and shook his head. He deserved it. He had been awful to her and their two unborn children.

"I am sorry," Graham said looking into her eyes.

Graham didn't know if Bettie was going to shout, moan or even hit him. But she started smiling and Graham felt his eyes start to drip, until now he hadn't realised how badly he had missed Bettie. He had missed out much about her, her smile and the two amazing people inside her.

"I am so, so sorry," Graham said.

Bettie smiled. "I know you are. But we have a case,"

Graham grinned at her. At least he finally had a chance to prove to her how sorry he was and how desperately he wanted to prove himself to her.

"Great. What is it?" Graham asked.

Bettie frowned.

Graham tried to look a bit less pleased. "Can I come home tonight?"

Bettie laughed. "Of course you idiot. I'm not that mad at you. And there's a reason we're here,"

Graham looked around and nodded. It was a bit weird she wanted to meet here.

"What do you know about the Electronic Robbery two weeks ago?" Bettie asked.

"Not a lot. Wasn't in my department at all, but I heard over a million pounds worth of Macs, phones and other laptops were stolen. Why?"

Bettie tried to get up a few times, but Graham wrapped his arms around her and helped her to her feet.

"Thanks," Bettie said. "Because we're going to do what the cops couldn't. We're going to find out exactly what happened here, who stole the tech and most importantly we're going to get it back,"

Graham wasn't sure on that. From everything he had heard the best cops in Kent Police were on the case, he knew him and Bettie were great together. But he doubted they could do better on this case.

Then he realised he was missing a critical piece of information.

"Bettie, what is this place?" Graham asked.

Graham almost jumped when he saw Sean standing next to him.

Sean laughed. "Well Graham, this is where the stolen lorry was found with all the tech missing,"

Bettie nodded. "We need to find out what the cops missed, and where the thieves might have gone next,"

"You seriously think we'll find something the cops missed?" Graham asked.

Bettie and Sean smiled.

"My darling Graham," Bettie said, "we know we will. And that's a promise. We have a secret weapon after all,"

Now that got Graham's full attention.

CHAPTER 5
1st May 2020
Dover, England

Bettie was really looking forward to using Sean as their secret weapon in a moment, because after years of thinking Sean's degree was in computing. Sean had finally admitted it wasn't computing, but all he said was his true degree would be their secret weapon in this case.

Bettie just hoped he was right. Otherwise she was going to look really silly in front of Graham but she had really enjoyed scaring Graham like that.

It might have been cruel, unneeded and torturous to him, but after all the panic Graham had put her through in the last week in-between the extremely rare moments of her family's badgering and her investigating. Bettie wanted him to suffer a tiny bit.

And in all honesty, there was one extremely good reason why Bettie wanted to scare him. After everything, she just wanted to know how much he believed in what they were doing. She wanted to see if he was desperate to be a part of the family and make sure that she forgave him, and most importantly Bettie needed to know if Graham still loved her.

And thankfully he did.

So as Bettie stood in the centre of a horrible multi-storey car park with water dripping down, making a horrible noise, and the smell of urine and rotten birds and burnt weed in the air, Bettie wanted to start investigating.

Bettie hadn't looked at the case in any great detail yet, but she had the box file in Sean's car for later reading.

Yet it all turned out that the cops had managed to trace the stolen lorry to this car park. Bettie had to agree the concrete ceiling was definitely tall enough to fit a lorry, but it was strange how the car park had been abandoned for years.

Bettie could plainly see how dirty and disgusting the floor was with it being covered in leaves, dirt and more alarmingly pigeon feathers, so Bettie had been expecting there to be clear marks where people had driven in and out. Even the police vehicles should have left marks.

There were none.

"Auntie?" Sean asked.

Bettie turned around to see him crouched on the floor holding a piece of broken twig and he was poking something. Bettie really hoped it wasn't a dead bird or something.

That would be disgusting.

Bettie went over to him. "What you found?"

Graham came over too.

Bettie crouched down next to Sean and was surprised to see he was poking at something rubbery.

"Graham," Bettie said, "go back to the car please and bring us the file on the multi-storey. I want to know exactly what the cops did here,"

Graham nodded and ran off.

"He really wants you to forgive him," Sean said, quietly.

"I already have and he knows it. He just wants to make me really know," Bettie said.

"He loves you a lot," Sean said.

Bettie nodded as she poked the rubbery thing and moved some of the dirt, dust and leaves around it.

Bettie shook her head when she saw it was a sheet of rubber. It was probably the size of a4 paper, but this made no sense whatsoever.

Why would there be a sheet of rubber here?

Sean carefully picked it up. "This is brand new?"

"Here you go," Graham said.

"Thanks. Read it out for us please," Bettie said.

Graham nodded and flicked through it.

"Right," he said. "The police searched this floor. They found the lorry and that was their sole focus because they deemed the rest of the crime scene too contaminated to yield any value,"

Bettie rolled her eyes. They had only been here

twenty minutes and they had proved them wrong.

"And with the tech stolen and not here, the cops wanted to focus on missing that," Graham said.

Bettie could only nod to that. She couldn't blame them, that's exactly what Bettie would have done. But clearly that was a massive error on everyone's part.

"What's this secret weapon then Bet?" Graham asked.

Bettie stood up and looked at Sean. "So, what's your degree really in?"

"I thought it was in computers," Graham said.

Bettie nodded.

Sean stood up. "Nope. I take a lot of computer classes but that's Harry's degree. My degree's in Advanced Technological Engineering,"

Bettie's mouth dropped. She had no idea what that meant, but she felt like she was going to learn a lot.

"All you need to know about that is I get to play with drones and I create software for them," Sean said, as he went to the boot of the car and found the condom Graham had sat on.

Bettie was rather horrified when Sean gave a schoolboy smile at it and then threw it away. It clearly came from a particularly good night.

"Here," Sean said, as he bought out a small expensive drone that Bettie had seen in tech shops.

Graham gasped, and at least Bettie knew what to get him for his birthday. She wondered how long until he started drooling over it.

Sean took out his phone, turned on the drone and it started whirling as it flew up.

"I created this piece of software last term for some coursework," Sean said, gesturing Bettie and Graham to stand next to him.

Bettie went over to him and smiled when she saw the drone was projecting a video feed to his phone. Then she was really impressed when she noticed the drone was picking out little indentations, markings and other features in the dirt.

"Is that reading the ground?" Graham asked.

"Yea," Sean said. "The drone is scanning the entire floor as we speak. It should be able to detect objects in the ground within five centimetres which in this car park I doubt will be a problem,"

Bettie hugged him. This was amazing and extremely impressive. If this worked, she was definitely going to write a letter of commendation to his Head of School at the university. Sean deserved to be praised for this real-world achievement.

"What's that?" Graham asked, pointing to something on the screen.

Bettie watched Sean zoom in on his phone and it looked like there was something long and thin under the dirt on the far side of the car park.

Bettie quickly walked over and stopped when she found the drone hovering over a large pile of leaves.

"Is this it?" Bettie shouted at Sean.

Sean gave her a thumbs up.

Bettie slowly started to kick the leaves away, and

she was definitely right in her suspicions about beating the cops in finding something.

She was staring at a large cupboard box that once belonged to a Mac.

This was proof that the tech had once been here but what excited Bettie more was it was easy to get fingerprints from boxes.

And Bettie really hoped there were some.

CHAPTER 6
1ˢᵗ May 2022
Canterbury, England

Graham had never understood why he wasn't allowed in the crime labs so he could actually look at the evidence being studied and tested and whatever else the Forensic people did, but he supposed that he just had to make do.

At least this time Senior Forensic Specialist Zoey Quill had been nice enough to let Graham sit in her little boxroom office whilst she finished up a few tests for him. He had tried to get Bettie in here too but Zoey had firmly said no.

As much as they all got on and enjoyed working with each other, as far as the world was concerned Bettie was not a cop, she was just a pretender. And no civilians whatsoever were allowed in the crime labs.

That was just unfair.

As Graham sat on one of the two soft wooden chairs in Zoey's office that sat perfectly in front of her large messy desk with almost mathematical precision, the smell of sweet flowers, old coffee and even some lemony cleaning chemicals all combined into a rather wonderful aroma. Graham didn't know if he would go so far as to say it was an amazing smell that he would like to smell all day, but it came pretty close.

The sounds of forensic people talking, glass bottles being pushed around and the creaking wheels of trolleys (probably with dead bodies) filtered into the office from the corridor outside.

And just as Graham was about to get up and have a look outside, Zoey walked in with a massive smile on her face. She wore her normal long white lab coat that framed her tall elegant body and pretty face perfectly, there always was something rather attractive about Zoey.

But Graham only ever had eyes for Bettie. He wished she was here for this part.

Zoey sat down her at her desk and pulled up the results on her computer.

"Detective Adams," Zoey slowly said, "you are the only Detective in the police force that brings me weird gifts,"

Graham leant closer at that comment. "What's so strange about some rubber and a cardboard box from a Mac?"

Zoey smiled. "You told me that you're investigating the theft from a few weeks ago. The one involving over 1 million pounds of tech, right?"

Graham nodded. Everyone should have known that, everyone was rather surprised when the Police Captain told them publicly that Graham was taking over the case.

"Well," Zoey said, "this Mac box didn't come from that theft. It came from another theft up in Yorkshire,"

Graham just shook his head at that. Why the hell would someone steal a bunch of Macs from Yorkshire in the far north of England and then steal some more all the way down here?

"I assume-" Graham said.

"Yes. I contacted my old friend who works in Hull with the police there. Turns out a shipment of high tech computers were stolen when they were delivered Hull Port. They were never found and the police dropped the case after two days,"

"Why?" Graham asked.

"Because the police in the North aren't as well funded as us. You know the North-South Divide in England. They didn't have the resources to keep up an investigation with no leads,"

Graham shook his head. That was definitely one of the downsides about England, there was definitely a richer south than the North, and he really hoped that would change in time.

"What did the insurance company say?" Graham asked.

Zoey smiled. "You're going to like this one. That shipment was insured by Fishers Insurance, the same company Bet's working for now,"

Graham laughed a little at that. It was too strange that two similar shipments, being insured by the same company goes missing days or a week apart. Someone was using that company as a hitlist or someone wanted to destroy them.

"That's great. Thanks," Graham said. "What about fingerprints?"

Zoey looked up at the ceiling and sort of shook her head. "That's where this gets even stranger,"

"Why?"

"Because the box was too clean. I can't even tell you if the box ever contained a computer or was even touched by a machine,"

Graham bit his lip. That was very strange indeed, and considering Zoey couldn't find something. Graham definitely believed there was nothing, Zoey was that good.

"Okay," Graham said. "What about the rubber sheet?"

Zoey shot up. She was excited.

"That was amazing! Turns out it's a new synthetic type of rubber. Cheaper to produce, more eco-friendly and it survives higher temperatures too. I read about it in the *British Journal of Forensics* last month,"

As much as Graham didn't want to know why rubber was being mentioned in an academic journal, he had to ask.

"Why?"

"Because there are lots of new applications of this new rubber. One, new forensic gloves can be made from it. Two, we can coat our glass beakers in it and heat them up more without the glass cracking. Three, they can be used to cool a computer down,"

Graham nodded. At least all this was starting to paint a picture, he just didn't know what the whole picture was yet. But he couldn't understand why these thieves would need so many computers and need to cool them down so much?

"How would rubber cool down computers?" Graham asked.

"It's simple really. If you…" Zoey trailed off with a massive smile and she typed away at her laptop.

All Graham could see was she was searching for a specific chemical.

"Care to share?" Graham asked.

"This new type of rubber. If you combine it with a certain chemical then it becomes an extreme cheap super coolant, so it could be impossible for tons of computers to overheat,"

Graham clicked his fingers. "You're checking to see if anyone has made large purchases recently,"

Zoey nodded then frowned. "Nope. No one in Kent has made any purchases,"

Graham grinned slightly. "And that is where forensics meets police work. This chemical is mainly made up North, and I have access to those purchase orders, you don't,"

Zoey smiled. "Always happy to help,"

"Thank you," Graham said, leaving the office.

He had to make a few calls.

He had to find out if anyone bought that chemical recently.

Graham really hoped the case was about to shatter open.

And that excited him far more than he ever thought possible.

CHAPTER 7
1st May 2022
Canterbury, England

After Graham had told Bettie this so-called case shattering idea, Bettie quickly realised the only thing getting shattered was Graham's idea.

As Bettie sat at her large wooden desk in her office with Sean in a chair in front of her, she had finished requesting, emailing and going through the various purchase reports from the various chemical companies.

No one suspicious had a large amount of the chemicals needed to combine with the rubber to create the super-coolant.

Bettie pushed her chair away from her desk and gently leaned back, resting her hands on her baby bump. She was not impressed that they couldn't find anyone, but it meant that the criminals were clever, and that was only showed by the crimes themselves.

In all the thefts Bettie had worked on previously

there was some kind of mistake that thieves had made. Sometimes they had left a fingerprint, other times they had left a footprint or simply they had targeted the wrong place.

And there had to be a mistake here and Bettie just had to find it.

But as the wonderful smell of evening meals, roast dinners and pasta dishes from the Italian across the road started to filter through the open window, Bettie wasn't sure if she was going to crack it tonight.

She wanted to try.

That amazing Italian food was the best she had ever smelt, and she could almost taste the velvety, juicy tomato sauce, succulent meatballs and smooth pasta on her tongue. She needed some of that food.

Bettie just hoped there was some vegan stuff.

Then there was a knock on the door and Graham kept in. Bettie had really missed his handsome face and his sexy slim body.

"Sean, run across the high street for me and get us some dinner please," Bettie said, handing him her bank card.

Graham almost looked horrified.

"Come on Graham. It's not like he's going to lose it or buy too much," Bettie said.

Sean smiled. "Yea Graham, it's not like I'm going to spit on your food just for not trusting me,"

Graham mockingly hit him on the head as Sean left, and then he sat down.

"You know he will spit on your food now,"

Bettie said, half-joking.

"Any purchases?" Graham said.

Bettie grinned as he ignored the question. "None. All purchasers are normal, long term customers and even the people buying it regularly in small amounts all check out,"

Graham rolled his eyes.

"You know," Bettie said, "our thieves probably stole it. They've been stealing everything else,"

Graham leant forward. "Have they?"

Bettie cocked her head. She had never thought of that.

"You think they didn't steal the rubber?" Bettie asked.

Graham nodded.

Bettie looked up the rubber on her laptop. "Looks like the rubber is made here in Canterbury by a local firm. But this is interesting, the company is only made up of ten people,"

Graham shrugged. "That's interesting because…"

"Because how could ten people find enough money to create this rubber," Bettie said.

It was a good point and the only thing Bettie could think of was there was an outside investor. Then that raised two more questions for her, who was the investor? And why hadn't the company been bought out by a large tech firm yet?

From everything Sean had been telling her about these small companies, she was surprised most of them hadn't been bought out already.

It seemed like the mega-companies liked to invest and monitor smaller companies to stop them from being better than themselves.

The door opened as Sean came back in holding a bag full of takeaway containers and pizza boxes. He passed a large pizza box to Bettie. She opened it and instantly smiled as she smelt the best Vegan BBQ chicken pizza she had ever smelt.

It was to die for.

"Thanks," Bettie said. "Sean quick question, would a larger tech firm invest secretly into a small 10 person company?"

Sean nodded. "Course. It needs to be secret so their competitors don't invest and buy out the smaller company before them,"

Bettie just looked at Graham. "I think there are two things we need to look into. We need to investigate the company's employees that created the rubber. That way we know if the thieves got it legally or stole it,"

Everyone nodded.

"Then," Bettie said, "we need to double check who's interested in this company,"

"Why?" Sean asked.

"We need to make sure this interested person isn't stealing from the company. What better way to learn the company's weakness than to be pretend to be an investor," Bettie said.

"And if you steal that rubber," Sean said, "you

can sell it to a larger tech company and make a fortune,"

Bettie nodded.

Graham finished a slice of pizza. "What about Fishers Insurance? Did they know about the theft in Hull?"

Bettie nodded. "I'm about to go and see Madeline now. She lives in Rochester. So me and Sean won't be gone long,"

With that, the three of them gathered up their takeaway containers and pizza boxes and prepared to eat on the move, this was going to be a late night.

But an extremely exciting one.

And Bettie was thrilled about that.

CHAPTER 8
1st May 2022
Canterbury, England

Despite the sun setting a few minutes ago, Graham loved the wonderfully warm night air with amazing hints of fresh pine, mint and sweet flowers mixing together as he walked up a little concrete pathway to the black front door of the owner of the Ultimate Rubber Company.

To Graham a company with a name like that sounded like some dodgy fetish business rather than a so-called respectable rubber research and development company. But Graham was hardly going to judge anyone at all, and certainly not by their name.

Especially considering he hated his own name at times. Graham made him sound so old and like he was born very early in the last century, he was only mid-thirties.

Graham stopped outside the black front door and admired the golden door frame, knocker and letter box. This might have seemed strange to other people but in his experience, you could always tell how rich someone was by judging their door. It was the first thing someone saw after the front garden.

And considering how maintained and great looking the garden was, Graham was hardly surprised to see a coating of real gold on the front door. This guy clearly had some money.

Jude Turner had started the company five years ago with the mission of creating a brand new type of rubber that would transform the world. Graham always admired people with big ambition, and whilst Jude had failed a few times (but he made a killing in the fetish market for the first two years of the business to make cash), Jude had kept his ambition.

And judging by everything he saw now, Graham was more than inclined to believe his ambition was paying off.

Graham knocked on the door.

A few moments later, a very small thin woman opened the door that only came up to Graham's waist. He wanted to guess it was a child, but it clearly wasn't judging by the furious stare he was getting from her.

"Yes I am a tiny person," she said.

"I'm sorry," Graham said.

"Na. It's fine. I get it a lot. Who are ya? What ya want?"

"I'm Detective Adams Kent Police. I'm looking for your... I'm looking for Jude Turner. Does he live here?"

The woman laughed. "Not for much longer. He ain't here yet. Come on in and I'll make you a coffee,"

Graham licked his lips when she said that, it had been ages (this morning) since he had one. He hated drinking them around Bettie because she couldn't have one. He always tried to respect her and not make her jealous.

Graham went into the house and the little woman led him past small box rooms, two bedrooms and a very large living room. He had no idea how big the house was from outside.

Then they both entered a very modern kitchen with marble worktops, a kitchen island in the middle with chairs and a very large copper oven. Graham loved the shiny coppery look of the oven. He might have to have a look for one when he got home.

The woman gestured for Graham to take a seat. He did, and he was surprised by the comfortableness of the chairs.

"Why you want to see Jude?" the woman asked.

"Who are you?" Graham asked.

"I'm his girlfriend. Leah Hall. Been dating him on and off for five years ever since he started that damn company,"

"You don't like it?"

"Na cop. He met me in a bar one night saying how he was going to be famous, rich and all-powerful. He bought me home and I liked him. A month later he comes begging me for money, so I give it to him. He loses, asks again and I say no. I work damn hard for my money,"

Graham really didn't want to get on the wrong side of Leah.

"Then I find out," Leah said, "he entered the fetish business. I ain't fussy about sex, but he pretends he has so-called morals and everything. And that I was disgusting for wanting to try out some of the products he was making!"

Graham didn't know what to say. She was right, it was a little weird that he didn't want to share this stuff. But Graham wasn't going to tell her that.

"Do you know anything about any investors?" Graham asked.

Leah poured the boiling water into two mugs and added the instant coffee.

"Ya know what cop. You might be onto something, he did come into a lot of cash three years ago and he's been damn well obsessed with that garden ever since,"

Graham nodded. That was even strange. A person obsessed with a garden. Money problems. Then a strange mystery investor turns up.

"What this about?" Leah asked, as she gave Graham his coffee.

It smelt amazing.

"Do you know of any thefts lately? Tech thefts specifically?" Graham asked.

"What?" Leah asked. "Like the one on the news few weeks ago about the Macs and tech?"

Graham nodded.

"Na. Besides the news," Leah said.

Graham was about to roll his eyes when Leah banged her mug on the island. It was times like this that he wished his beautiful Bettie was here.

"Now ya mention it. Jude was very nervous about it. Did... did he steal them? It would make sense?"

"Shut up woman!" a man shouted.

Graham got off the chair and stared at a very angry looking middle-aged man wearing a very wet coat, boots and black trousers. It was clearly raining outside now.

Great! Graham didn't bring a coat with him.

"Jude?" Graham asked.

"Yea," he said.

"Detective Adams, Kent Police," Graham said, moving carefully towards him.

"I need to ask you a few questions about your company,"

Jude frowned. "What company? I don't run it. She does,"

Graham frowned.

Spun around.

Leah smashed a mug into his head.

Graham fell to the floor.

Whacking his head too.

His world went black.

CHAPTER 9
1st May 2022
Canterbury, England

The only thing Bettie didn't like about wonderful houses that were owned by the rich, rich was how they made her feel completely inadequate.

Now Bettie was never ever going to be a housewife but as her and Sean walked into Madeline's massive kitchen with a very high copper coloured ceiling and large light bulbs hanging down. Bettie was really starting to feel like her house was awful.

Even Madeline's worktops were expensive black and gold marble that stretched on for ten, twenty metres and she had all of the latest gadgets and equipment and everything that a rich person could ever want.

And unlike tons of the other rich people, Bettie had worked with before, Madeline actually worked her kitchen as Bettie could smelt the most sensational, buttery and warningly spiced curry filling the entire kitchen. It wasn't overpowering or disgusting, it was just right.

Madeline wearing (what normal people considered overdressed) her long silk white robe, pearl necklace and made-up smiled at Bettie and Sean as she popped up on the kettle and gestured them to take a seat.

Bettie was surprised that the massively long worktop was actually part of an immense kitchen island with see through glass chairs underneath, so they all took a seat.

Madeline passed Sean and herself some richly spiced black coffee, and Bettie had some flavoured tea.

She would have preferred the other drink, but it was only a few more months to go.

"You wanted to know something?" Madeline asked, her voice posh and without a hint of fatigue.

"Yes," Bettie said, "you never told me about a theft of computer equipment in Hull,"

Madeline looked at the ceiling like she was struggling to remember that theft.

"Oh," she said. "I never dealt with that. Hunter mentioned it to me but because we all have equal shares of the company, he doesn't need my permission to do anything. I presume he dealt with the theft himself,"

Bettie and Sean just looked at each other.

"That's a bit strange," Sean said.

Bettie nodded.

"I know. It isn't ideal," Madeline said. "The business was originally me, the Lewis' and my husband. He died a year ago, brain cancer and in spite of everything I did for him. He transferred his share of the company to the Lewis' so we are all in equal control,"

"I'm sorry for your loss," Bettie and Sean said.

"Don't be. I hate him for what he did about his shares. It's my company and… I'm sorry. I just have no one to vent to about these sorts of things,"

Bettie gently placed her hand on Madeline's arm and rubbed it gently.

"What do you need to know about the Hull claim?" Madeline said, as she got out her phone and presumably pulled up the records.

"Any details please. Who owned the tech? Who got the insurance money? Everything?" Bettie said.

Madeline swore under her breath and gave Bettie her phone.

Bettie let Sean get closer. She couldn't believe that the insurance paperwork said it had been handled and Eagle Computers (the company who's tech was stolen) had received half a million pounds in compensation. But then there were later emails from the company asking where their money was.

Bettie passed the phone back to Madeline. "You think Hunter stole the money?"

Madeline's eyebrows rose. "I couldn't be surprised. I actually caught him once. It was about three years ago,"

"Why steal?" Sean asked.

"He said it was for some investment opportunity but he never said what, and he returned the money," Madeline said.

Bettie cocked her head. An investment opportunity? She knew it was a real shot in the dark, but there was a remote chance that Hunter Lewis was the mysterious investor behind The Ultimate Rubber Company (that was such a stupid name).

But Bettie didn't know how Hunter could do it?

From everything she knew about research and development, it wasn't cheap. Especially if Hunter wanted this Jude someone to create a brand new type of Rubber, Bettie hated to think how much money it would cost.

Probably in the millions.

So how did Hunter Lewis get the money?

That's even if he actually was the investor.

"Auntie," Sean said tapping Bettie on the shoulder.

Bettie was about to moan at him when she realised she must have been in deep thought about the question.

"Have you ever heard of The Ultimate Rubber Company?" Bettie asked.

Madeline nodded. "Of course. It's a client of ours. He insured their property and their buildings and I think we insured the owner's life as part of a new trial we're doing,"

Sean leant forward. "Who's life? Jude Turner?"

Madeline's eyebrows rose. "Who's Jude Turner? The Ultimate Rubber Company is owned by Leah Hall,"

Bettie sat back. That made no sense, all the official paperwork said Jude was in charge. Why have the real owner of the company a secret?

"Thanks," Bettie said, as she dialled Graham.

He might as well know and not look like an idiot in front of Jude Turner.

He didn't answer.

She tried again. He might have been driving.

He didn't answer.

She tried again.

It didn't even dial.

If this had happened last week, Bettie wouldn't have been concerned in the slightest. She knew that Graham was scared about having twins, but she knew that he wanted to prove himself to her.

Graham wouldn't avoid her phone calls even if he wanted a bit of me-time.

Something was wrong.

"Sean. Call Graham. Now," she said.

Sean nodded and dialled Graham.

Nothing.

Bettie felt her stomach twist as she knew that something was extremely wrong.

Graham was missing.

And now Bettie had to save the man she loved.

CHAPTER 10
1st May 2022
Canterbury, England

Graham opened his eyes, but he hated that he couldn't see anything. All he could see was a very thin line of light at the very bottom of his vision.

He tried to move his wrists and stand up.

Sharp pain ripped into his wrists and ankles, and Graham instantly knew that he was tied up. Probably to a wooden chair given how cold he felt as he ran his restricted fingers across a hard surface.

As much as Graham's body, heart and mind wanted to panic and lash out at the world for daring to endanger him when he had two children on the way. Graham forced himself to take long slow breaths of the coffee-scented air.

Graham didn't know why Leah Hall had felt the need to knock him out. He was only going to ask her a few questions, because if he had learnt anything about companies during his time on the police force, it was there were so many legal loopholes that innocent people could use for various reasons.

Right up to the point where Leah knocked him out, Graham didn't have any reason to suspect she was doing anything criminal.

Now Graham wasn't so sure.

"You just attacked a pig?" Jude said.

Graham was a bit offended by that horrible term, but he wanted to see if he could make his captors angry at each other.

"I know that," Leah said. "We need to run. Have you got everything?"

"Yep,"

Graham shook his head. He had heard his phone ringing earlier so he hoped that Bettie and Sean were worried and coming to get him. Thankfully Graham was still in their house (he hoped), so all Bettie needed to do was come here and free him.

He just hoped Leah and Jude wouldn't hurt them.

"Question," Graham said.

"For fuck sake!" Leah shouted. "You said the cop was going to sleep through the night. We need to run now,"

Graham just shook his head. "I wasn't going to arrest you, you know,"

He heard footsteps getting closer.

Leah ripped tape off his eyes.

Graham hissed as he swore his eyebrows had been ripped off.

"What pig?" Jude asked.

Graham smiled. "I only wanted to know about an a4 piece of rubber that your company made,"

Both Jude and Leah looked at each other.

"A4?" Leah asked.

Graham nodded.

"How you know that pig?"

Graham really didn't like Jude.

"We found it at a crime scene. A bunch of tech was stolen," Graham said.

"We?" Leah said, clearly annoyed.

"He has friends coming here now," Jude said. "I'm leaving,"

Graham and Leah both watched Jude run out of the house and then Leah just looked at Graham.

"I guess I won't be seeing him again," Leah said, picking up a large knife.

Graham tensed and focused on the knife.

"Oh," Leah said, exchanging glances with the knife and Graham. "I'm so sorry. Um,"

Leah came over to Graham and cut him free. Then she put the knife in the sink far away from either one of them.

"You weren't going to arrest me?" Leah asked.

Graham folded his arms. "That was before you knocked me out,"

Leah bit her lip and looked at the floor.

"But answer my questions. Then we have a deal, and I won't arrest you,"

Leah's eyes narrowed. "Fine,"

"How did a piece of A4 rubber from your company get to my crime scene?" Graham asked.

Leah picked up a mug of coffee from the worktop and sipped it.

"That's why we knocked you out," Leah said. "The company… it's failing. We have an investor we don't even know buying it out from under us. We'll lose the company in days. So we *borrowed* from it,"

Graham smiled. "It isn't stealing if it's your own company,"

Leah laughed. "The Investor wouldn't see it like that. I took a box of our Rubber and sold it on the Dark Web. Each sheet sold for five grand,"

Graham's mouth dropped. Even if there was only ten sheets in each box that's a fifty thousand pound payday.

"Did you sell it all to one person?" Graham asked.

Leah nodded. "I technically broke at least two laws. Am I going to jail?"

Graham cocked his head. He didn't think Leah or even Jude were really bad people, they were just trying to make some money as their business was taken from them.

That got Graham thinking.

"Wait, you said the Investor was taking the business from you. How?"

Leah folded her arms. "That bastard was spreading rumours about us. Making lies about us. And stealing our stock,"

Graham smiled. "Stealing stock?"

"Yep," Jude said, walking back in.

Graham doubted he ever actually left.

"We were meant to get a shipment of natural rubber every Monday," Leah said. "Every other week the shipment would disappear from us. Then the Investor would ransom the shipment for us,"

Graham smiled and started to walk out of the house. He now fully believed that the Investor was the criminal mastermind behind all of this, but he couldn't help but feel like he was walking into something much, much bigger than he realised.

And that excited him.

But he felt like he was missing a critical piece of the puzzle too.

When he got to the front door, he saw Bettie and Sean marching up the driveaway. Bettie looked furious.

But pleased to see him.

Bettie was about to say something. Graham waved her silent.

"It's a long story. But I know who we're looking for," Graham said.

A VERY URGENT MATTER

CHAPTER 11
2nd May 2022
Canterbury, England

For a chance Bettie was rather surprised with herself as she watched Sean finishing putting up the chalkboard in her office, and Graham wrote up the facts of the case so far.

Bettie had never really liked chalkboards or going this old fashioned, but if there was never a case that demanded such things. It was definitely this case, but Bettie couldn't believe how excited she was that she was going to be investigating a criminal mastermind.

That was going to be great fun.

As Bettie sat on her desk next to a wonderful plate of vegan Danish pastries that Sean and Harry had bought in before Harry went to a lecture. Bettie had really liked seeing Sean and Harry together in person, because it really made something clear as day to her.

The two boyfriends really made Bettie realise

how much she loved Graham. And she was never that annoyed at him for leaving or running off in the first place, because she understood the urge so well.

And she was jealous. Bettie was jealous that he had had the courage to run away and find some alone time and she hadn't been. Bettie had forced herself to be surrounded by her nagging family, her work and whatever else she had wanted to do.

When in reality, Bettie could have made some alone time for herself so she could process what having twins meant to her.

And Graham did have a great ass as he bend down to write something on the bottom of the chalkboard.

Bettie damn well loved that man.

"What do we know about the Investor?" Sean asked, pretending to be Sherlock Holmes.

Bettie almost laughed at the idea of a gay Sherlock Homes.

"We know they invested in The Ultimate Rubber Company," Bettie said, trying not to laugh at the stupid name.

"Then," Graham said, "the Investor went around stealing shipment, ransoming the company and making sure they sold it to him or her,"

Bettie cocked her head. "They were selling? I thought you said they were-"

"They had no choice. The Investor was stealing the business right from under them. Best to sell in two days and get some money. Then none at all,"

Bettie nodded at that. It sounded perfectly logical and that was what was annoying her about this mystery person. They seemed to be too logical and too well informed about exactly how to destroy a business.

"What about the person who Leah sold the rubber to?" Bettie asked.

Graham shook his head. "It's the Dark Web Bet. No one is traceable there if they were clever. Leah tried to trace them but she came up with nothing,"

"What about Hunter?" Sean asked, pointing to his picture on the board.

Bettie smiled. "He did steal from Fisher Insurance three years ago,"

"About the time someone solved Jude's money problems," Graham said.

"And he would have known about the shipments of tech, and when the shipments of rubber were coming in," Sean said.

"How?" Graham asked.

"Because," Bettie said, "for some reason each shipment needed to be insured individually and Fishers Insurance needed to be told,"

Just saying that made Bettie suspicious of it all. Her mother had worked in insurance for decades and she had never mentioned something as complex as that, granted Bettie's mother worked in building insurance. But surely the principles were the same?

Begging the question why did Fishers Insurance want to be notified of everything?

Sean took out his phone and nodded to Bettie. She was rather pleased Madeline had given him her phone number last night.

Bettie went over to Graham and stood so close to him that she could feel all his wonderful body heat. He gave a schoolboy smile.

"I'm glad you're back," Bettie said.

"Me too," Graham said, kissing her.

"Cough, cough," Sean said, grinning.

Bettie wrapped her arms round Graham and looked at Sean.

"Madeline said it isn't their policy and all customers know that. She believes that is something Hunter Lewis does for the policy customers he oversees,"

Bettie grabbed Hunter's picture off the chalkboard.

"So we have an executive at the company who steals, knows about the stolen shipments and makes the customer tell him when one is coming in. I think we have a suspect,"

Graham shook his head. "But how did Hunter Lewis have the money to invest in all these companies. Leah emailed he saying the Investor invested over £5 million into their company. I doubt Hunter had that sort of money,"

Sean picked up a Danish and walked over pointing to the wife, Eva Lewis.

"Have we looked into her yet?" he said.

Bettie smiled. No they hadn't.

Bettie went over to her laptop and ran a quick background search on Eva Lewis, starting with the all important financials.

Bettie swore under her breath as she read the reports. "She doesn't have that sort of money at all,"

Graham frowned. "Hunter and Eva Lewis are the most likely…"

Bettie smiled at Graham. "What you thinking?"

"Sean," Graham said, "if you were going to attack an insurance company. How would you do it?"

"You rinse them dry," he said.

"Or?" Graham said.

Bettie waved her hand. "Or you go after their clients and then you can make them lose clients and rinse them of money at the same time,"

Graham nodded.

Bettie stood in front of the board and folded her arms.

"That's what this is all about. This is a campaign to get rid of Fishers Insurance and I think we need to talk to the Lewis's. I don't think they're the criminals here. I think they're victims,"

Bettie smiled as she heard Graham and Sean grunt.

"Think about it. The Investor has stolen shipments. Infiltrated companies. Forced company owners to sell their business. If they really wanted to destroy Fishers Insurance, what better way than to force Hunter and Eva to do it for them?"

Sean and Graham nodded.

"We need to go and see them," Graham said.
Bettie couldn't agree more.

CHAPTER 12
2nd May 2022
Dover, England

Given what Bettie had told Graham about the grandeur of Madeline's house, he had been expecting the same sort of thing from Hunter and Eva Lewis's house.

He was flat out wrong.

As the couple guided him, Bettie and Madeline into a dirty dark little room that had a TV standing (barely) in one corner, Graham had to presume this was their excuse of a living room. The so-called family heart of the home.

Graham would have hated to grow up here, he hated how dark and unloved and almost evil this place felt. When the twins were born, he was going to make sure their home never looked or felt like this disgusting place.

Two mugs of tea were smashed accidentally onto the coffee table in front of them, and as much as the

Lewises were gesturing Graham and Bettie to sit down. They both looked at each other, and Graham realised neither one of them was brave enough.

Graham was almost glad Sean had to talk with a lecturer about an upcoming exam, at least he didn't have to endure this living room. It even stunk of mouldy teabags, food and other horrible smells.

"You wanted to see us before we went into work?" Eva said, looking concerned.

Bettie carefully sat down on the sofa and stared at Eva.

"We requested the visit," she said, coldly.

Madeline gestured to her friends she didn't know the reason for this, and she was right. It had been Bettie's idea not to tell her anything. They both wanted to see all of their reactions.

"We know," Graham said, "that you have been supplying customer shipment details to someone else,"

"What!" Madeline shouted.

"We also know," Bettie said, "that you are being blackmailed or something into helping this person,"

Graham was surprised to see neither Eva nor Hunter were showing any sign of relief or even annoyance. Graham wouldn't like to face them in a poker game, that's of course if he could actually play poker.

Madeline stood up. "How dare you both steal from me, our customers and my husband,"

Eva laughed. "Seriously? Like your husband ever

cared about you. He was right, you are just an old prune,"

Graham gasped.

"How did you know?" Madeline said.

Graham was rather surprised she would admit that.

"Come on, you really think we worked late every night. He spent his evenings with me! I was fun! Interesting! Exciting! I wasn't an *old prune*,"

Graham now wished he had bought popcorn.

"You slept with my husband!" Madeline shouted.

"And he fucked me good," Eva said, storming out.

But when Graham looked down at Hunter he was smiling, he didn't seem to care in the slightest that his wife had just revealed an affair.

Bettie pointed at him. "You knew. You didn't stop it. You... were glad,"

Hunter grinned and then pointed to some pictures on the walls behind them. Graham noticed there were three young, very cute children playing with Eva on their bed, at theme parks and just doing all the kid things that loving families did together.

Graham smiled. He was really looking forward to those times.

"You aren't the father," Graham said.

Hunter shook his head. "I couldn't. Eva got with Madeline's husband and... nine months later... we had triplets,"

Now Graham was firmly glad he was only having

twins, and judging by Bettie's loud gasp and crossing of her legs. She was glad to.

"I'm sorry Made," Hunter said.

"I'm sorry too," Eva said, coming back in. "It's just... we wanted kids so, so bad,"

Madeline's lips thinned but she eventually smiled.

Bettie waved her hands in the air. "Some people found out, didn't they?"

Hunter looked at Eva frowning.

"Yes," Eva said. "I got letters and photos and DNA test results for god sake. They all came last month. They threatened us with Madeline finding out, them going to the papers and making this all a local and even national scandal,"

Graham cocked his head. "How?"

Eva laughed nervously. "My parents were never rich growing up. I was dumped on the streets at 15 so I had to... use my body to get by,"

Graham vowed to never let them happen to his own children.

"So the blackmailer," Hunter said, "wanted to create a gripping headline. Dover Slut Hunts Down Local Lonely Man For Children,"

Graham laughed. "It isn't exactly catchy,"

Eva frowned. "It makes a point though, doesn't it?"

Graham stopped laughing and nodded.

Bettie went over to Eva and hugged her.

"Who could have found out? And do you have the letters and everything?"

Eva pushed away from Bettie and wiped her eyes.

"No," Hunter said, "things got strange. After a few days the reports, letter, everything dissolved,"

Graham and Bettie just looked at each other. Whoever the Investor was, they had to be one of the most skilled people Graham had ever come across.

First the forensically clean Mac box, then the Dark Web stuff and now the dissolving paper.

Graham clicked his fingers. "What if… the thefts aren't done by the Investor?"

Graham's and Bettie's and Madeline's eyes narrowed on Eva and Hunter.

"What if," Bettie asked, "the thefts were done to find the Investor?"

"How would that work?" Madeline asked.

Graham just looked at Eva and Hunter. "You know all the victims of the crimes. You know exactly who would want help getting their livelihoods back,"

Eva moved uncomfortably.

"Exactly," Bettie said, "you knew once we found out about the Investor. We could think they did the thefts. But you did, didn't you?"

Eva smiled. "You were meant to stop here,"

"Shut up," Hunter said.

"Hunter," Graham said. "The game is up but we might be able to help you out,"

Hunter and Eva held each other's hand. "How?"

"Tell us everything and we might be able to help you find out who the Investor is," Bettie said.

"And we won't go to jail?" Eva asked.

Bettie smiled at Graham. And after years of loving that beautiful sexy woman, Graham knew full well what that smile meant, and he wasn't going to refuse her.

"Fine Bet," Graham said, looking at Eva. "If you help us, we won't arrest you,"

Bettie punched the air. Graham hugged her quickly.

"I think though," Bettie said, "if we want to unmask a criminal mastermind. We might need certain Computer and Advanced Technological Engineer students,"

Graham smiled. That was a great idea and he was more than ready to make the phone call.

Graham knew if this was going to work. Then they needed all the help they could get.

CHAPTER 13
2nd May 2022

4 Miles Outside Dover, England

Bettie was flat out shocked when she entered a massive underground warehouse that stretched on for a good mile with hundreds of computers connected up to different machines.

This was amazing, and terrifying!

"Once we organised the drivers to deliver the goods to a pick-up good," Hunter said, "we would get the drivers to sign Non-Disclosure Agreements and then the two of us would transport the tech here,"

Bettie couldn't believe the vast scale of this warehouse, there must have been enough Macs and other computers here to hack into anywhere given how much computer power was already in each piece of tech.

Eva and Hunter led herself, Graham and the two love birds (Sean and Harry) into the depths of the warehouse, and Bettie was rather pleased that Sean and Harry constantly aweing and being shocked at all the different pieces of tech here.

Bettie didn't have a clue what some of these things attached to the computers were.

After a few minutes, Eva and Hunter led them to a massive central computer that was easily the height and width of Graham and it sat on a rather high tech looking platform.

And Bettie smiled when she noticed that tons of the A4 rubber sheets were attached to each computer and this main terminal.

"Please take a seat," Eva said.

Harry and Sean each took a seat at the main terminal and Bettie stared with awe at the impressiveness of the setup.

She was partly expecting the roar of the fans to cool down the computers to be deafening, but because of the rubber the fans weren't even needed.

"You think you can hack into the Investor?" Eva asked.

Bettie laughed. "Believe me, if there's something these two can't do with computers. Then it cannot be done,"

Bettie didn't know how true that was, but she loved both Harry and Sean enough to believe in them completely.

Hunter clicked his fingers. "Activating phrase 1 power up,"

The entire warehouse hummed slightly and Bettie felt the ground vibrate as hundreds of computers were powered on. Then everything went silent.

She looked at Eva but she was smiling so everything looked to be going well.

"Activating phrase 2," Hunter said, as he pressed a button.

Again the entire warehouse vibrated, with a pop and a bang as even more computers were powered up.

Bettie went over to Graham. "How long until the cops notice this energy surge?"

Graham frowned. "I fear not long,"

"Relax," Eva said, "all this runs on tidal, wind and solar power. We don't touch the main grid,"

Bettie smiled at that. At least this investigation wasn't harming the environment.

"Activating phrase 3," Hunter said.

The power went off.

"Shit!" Eva said.

The entire warehouse was bathed in red light and the main computer terminal turned off.

As much as Bettie wanted to believe it was just a mere power outage because of all the computers. She couldn't stop thinking about how smart and cunning the Investor had been.

Bettie couldn't shake the feeling he already knew about what they were doing.

"Auntie," Sean said, as him and Harry typed away at the main terminal.

"What?" Bettie said, coming over.

"During a research project, I created software

and a very detectable drone to knock out computers," Sean said.

Bettie really didn't like where this was going.

"The software unleashes a signal that computers detect and they start to read the code. Think of it as your phone reading a text message,"

Now Bettie seriously didn't like this.

"I think that same code here. This is my code," Sean said.

Harry hissed. "Babe, what you think of this?"

Sean looked at what Harry was doing. "Shit! Shit! Shit!"

"What?" Eva and Hunter asked.

Harry grinned. "Your Investor isn't hacking us. They're here in the building. I've seen computers malfunction like this before. This patterns of failure only happens when the attack is inside a building,"

Bettie and Graham looked at Eva and Hunter.

"Who knows about this place?" Bettie asked.

"We don't know," Eva said.

The power turned back on. Bettie didn't like that. It felt too easy.

"Shut it down!" Bettie shouted.

Hunter didn't.

Sean jumped up and raced over to the buttons Hunter was pressing.

Bang!

Sean was thrown metres back.

The buttons exploded.

Bettie and Harry rushed over. Harry wrapped his

arms around Sean.

Bettie checked for life signs. He was alive. Just unconscious.

"What the fuck!" Graham shouted.

Bettie spun around and frowned when she saw a white faceless mask was on the computer screen staring at them.

He had to be the Investor

Bettie laughed. "He must have used the power failure to get control of the computers,"

"Very clever Miss English," the Investor said.

"Why do this?" Harry shouted.

Bettie could have sworn the person was smiling behind the mask.

"Now everyone," the Investor said. "Are you ready to play a game?"

Bettie frowned. "Fuck off,"

She grabbed one of the chairs.

Throwing it into the main terminal.

The glass smashed.

Then every single computer in the warehouse turned on.

They all showed the Investor laughing.

It was deafening.

Bettie didn't know what she had done.

She didn't know how she would fix this.

Not a clue.

CHAPTER 14
2nd May 2022
4 Miles Outside Dover, England

Graham hated the Investor. He was going to end him!

Graham stared out at all the laughing computer screens that seemed to stretch on for miles upon miles. He knew that the Investor was here inside the building.

Eva, Hunter and Harry were making sure that Sean was okay despite him being unconscious. Graham had to make sure the Investor paid for that.

Dearly.

"You shouldn't have killed me my love!" the Investor shouted through the computer screens.

Intense humming and vibrating and popping filled the warehouse.

Graham and Bettie stared at Madeline.

"Who is this!" Graham shouted at Madeline.

She started to cry. Graham wasn't having it. It

was because of her they were in danger.

Graham had to help her. And save everyone.

"I don't know," Madeline said.

"She lies. She always lies!" the Investor said.

But Graham and Bettie looked at each other and smiled. That time the Investor's voice didn't sound like it was coming from a computer. The Investor was close.

So close that they could hear them over the computer noises.

"Who!" Graham shouted.

Madeline frowned. "I didn't mean to kill him. I didn't. I really didn't,"

A computer smashed on the floor.

Shattering.

Sending deadly glass shards through the air.

Slicing Madeline's cheek.

More computers flew towards them.

Graham jumped in front of Bettie.

No computers were being aimed at her.

They were all flying towards Madeline.

Graham spun around and protectively grabbed Bettie when he saw a very tall man wearing all black and a white faceless mask. He simply stood there, not speaking nor moving.

The computers hummed as loud as they could.

Tens of them exploded on the far side of the warehouse.

Electrical fires started.

The flames roared, crackled and popped.

Graham knew they were running out of time.

"Who are you?" Graham asked.

Graham heard someone run behind him.

The Investor whipped out their phone. Pressing a button.

"Ouch!" Harry shouted.

Graham quickly looked behind him to see harry holding his hand as if it had been electrocuted. Then he noticed Harry had been trying to reach the main terminal.

Maybe just because the screen was destroyed, it didn't mean that the computer controls were damaged.

"You are clever," the Investor said to Harry. "But you will not be accessing the fire procedures. I control everything,"

Graham just shook his head. This guy was dangerously smart, but who was he? Then Graham realised how the Investor referred to Madeline and a critical piece of information that Bettie had told him earlier.

"My love?" Graham asked to Madeline. "You told Bet you're husband died of brain cancer,"

The Investor laughed. "Oh. Did she now? I had the disease. I was cured of it. So she whacked me round the head with a spade and left me for dead. Pushed me off the white cliffs of Dover, didn't you know?"

Graham frowned at Madeline. "Tell me Madeline. Did your husband have a lot of money that he invested in other companies?"

Madeline looked like she was about to deny it, but she gasped and put her face in her hands.

The Investor typed in something else into his phone.

More computers exploded.

Bettie grabbed Graham's arm. "Remember this is all high-tech crimes. We're old school,"

Graham smiled at that. He loved Bettie more than anything else in the world. He was going to stop all this with amazing her.

All he needed to do was distract the Investor long enough for Bettie to do her magic.

Graham slowly started to walk away from Bettie.

"How did you survive?" Graham asked.

The Investor frowned and raised his phone into the air.

"I'm not stupid. Stop moving or I explode more tech," the Investor said.

"You know," Harry said, standing next to Graham, "this guy really is an... how do you English say it... oh yea idiot!"

Graham really hoped Harry (an Italian) knew what he was doing.

"I agree," Graham said.

The Investor ripped off his mask revealing an extremely horrible smashed up face with scars, burnt tissue and a collapsed in cheek covering all of it.

He was disgusting.

"This is what my bitch of a wife did to me!" the

Investor shouted.

"That what I mean," Harry said. "This guy is an idiot. In Italiana we don't plot secretly. That for cowards. We shoot them down in the street,"

Graham didn't know how to take that.

Graham took a few steps forward. The Investor put his fingers so close to his phone.

"One force move and I'll blow us all up!"

Graham laughed. "Come on. Even I know you aren't do that with computers. And come now Eva and Hunter Lewis are far more intelligent than you. That's why they trapped you,"

Graham loved lying to criminals.

The Investor looked so confused. He looked at his phone.

Then the entire warehouse went silent. All the computers switched off and the Investor stared at his phone as it went black.

Graham charged at him.

Tackling him to the ground.

Graham rolled the Investor onto his front and forced his arms behind his back.

"Mr Fisher I am arresting you on counts of blackmail, attempted murder, computer crimes and I am certain I can find more crimes to add to the list," Graham said.

"What about my bitch of a wife! She tried to fucking kill me!" he shouted.

Graham just looked over at Eva, Hunter and Madeline holding an unconscious Sean in their arms and putting him in the recovery position. And Bettie and Harry were who staring with massive frowns at the Investor.

"It's your word against hers," Graham said.

CHAPTER 15
2nd May 2022
Dover, England

As Graham watched younger police officers in full uniform take Mr Fisher away to be charged for his various crimes including the attempted murder of Graham and everyone else, various cybercrimes and blackmail. Graham just couldn't believe what Mr Fisher had said during the interrogation.

Graham didn't believe anything what he said about Madeline trying to kill him. It wasn't that Graham doubted that it happened, it clearly did, but he didn't believe it was all about money.

From the past two days and reading those newspaper reports about Madeline, she didn't seem the type of woman to only be interested in money. If anything else, it seemed that the Insurance company was her pride and joy, so more than likely it had been something to do with that.

But after Mr Fisher trying to kill Graham, Bettie

and the rest of them, Graham really didn't care too much.

As a cop, he should have arrested Madeline and brought her in for an interview. But why bother? She was hardly a threat to anyone and if anyone was to compare the two criminal's crimes. It wouldn't be hard to persuade jurors that Mr Fisher's crimes eclipsed Madeline's by millions of times over.

And if Graham was on the jury, he would have to agree.

As Graham started to walk out of the police station, through the multi-storey car park that smelt wonderful like freshly cut grass to his own large black car. He couldn't help but feel like this case was something that could have been avoided.

In the interview Mr Fisher had mentioned that he started to invest in companies three years ago because he wanted power, freedom and the ability to do whatever he wanted. From everything Graham knew about the Fishers, it sounded like Madeline was the one who needed to be freed.

Now Graham wasn't so sure.

It also turned out that Mr Fisher just wanted to ruin his millions so after he died of brain cancer, Madeline wouldn't be able to get any of it. And it didn't seem like Madeline cared too much, considering Graham had watched her donate all of the money to various charities after he arrested him.

But when Graham got to the most pressing of questions, he was rather shocked by the answer.

Graham had asked Mr Fisher why he started to steal the business from under the owner's feet. And Mr Fisher said because the voice told him to, and Graham didn't know what to make of it.

Of course he wouldn't have been surprised if Mr Fisher was crazy or suffered from some kind of mental health condition, but he hadn't encountered a voice before on cases.

And according to Mr Fisher (who was now getting extremely unreliable) after Madeline tried to kill him. The Voice had gotten louder and louder and louder, all to the point that he felt enslaved to it and he had to destroy his wife once and for all.

It was about that time that Graham had decided to call the interview over and he requested a psychologist to evaluate Mr Fisher.

From past experience, Graham knew that most of the criminals were lying about such things and mostly just used it as an excuse that was found out to be a lie by the time it got to trial. But the media still loved to shout and scream about it.

Yet even if there was a slim chance of Mr Fisher did have a condition, then for some reason Graham wanted him to be treated fairly by the legal system. Not because he would have wanted that on a personal or even a cop level, but because it was the right thing to do.

And that's why he was going to promise Bettie that he was never going anywhere. Graham loved Bettie and their two unborn twins more than anything else in the world, so Graham would never run off again and he would make sure that every decision about their lives was made together.

Because that's what Graham and Bettie were. A team. And a great one at that.

So as Graham got to his large black car, he popped open the car and really wanted to get back to Bettie's office, so he could tell her he loved her, treat her to a wonderful dinner and just prove to her how much she meant to him.

Because Bettie was truly the centre of Graham's world.

And it was a beautiful world at that.

CHAPTER 16
2nd May 2022
Canterbury, England

Bettie was extremely pleased to stand in her wonderful office and watch Sean and Harry walk hand in hand together down the amazing cobblestone high street of Canterbury.

The air smelt utterly stunning with hints of perfectly baked bread that would just melt into buttery deliciousness of her mouth, wonderful Italian food and tons of other amazing freshly baked pastries.

Bettie did truly love Canterbury. It didn't matter that it was May, spring or whatever. Bettie was always going to love Canterbury because it truly was such a magical place. It was filled with history, amazing people and more than enough mystery to keep her busy.

And she loved that.

Bettie kept watching Sean and Harry as they

walked back to the university and Bettie had to admit they really, really did make the perfect couple. They were sweet, cute and just perfect together.

And even when they were in the hospital checking that Sean was okay, Bettie was amazed how Harry was protecting him, comforting him and just being there for him.

Exactly how she would be there for Graham if anything happened to him, and she knew he would do the same for her. Because they were a team, a couple and partners.

Thankfully Sean was perfectly okay at the hospital, which made Bettie feel amazing and at least her sister Phryne (Sean's mother) wouldn't have to kill her just yet.

But Bettie was still surprised at how helpful Harry was. She had met him tons of times over the years since him and Sean started dating. Bettie loved Harry like she did Sean, but after this case… Bettie was definitely seeing him in a new light.

He was an Italian man, and that should have made Bettie realise it sooner. But he was the perfect person to have on her unofficial team, because Italians were all about family, like she was. And he was pretty good with a computer so Bettie would certainly have to make sure he was invited onto a case again.

It wasn't like Sean was going to be jealous.

When Bettie could no longer see the happy couple, she went over to her large wooden desk and closed her laptop. She had just been finishing up her report to Madeline after seeing a very handsome bank deposit into her account. It turned out that Bettie had received a great chunk of Mr Fisher's money.

Bettie was never going to complain there. It was probably enough to buy a few houses.

As Bettie sat down she was impressed with this case because if anything else, it showed her how much people don't like to be blackmailed, and they will always try to free themselves.

And as Bettie explained in her report, Eva and Hunter Lewis weren't bad people. They were just people who did the wrong things for the right reasons, they wanted to free themselves, Madeline and other companies from the Investor's corrupting touch.

So yes, they stole tons (and Bettie meant TONS) of computers, Macs and other electronics, and they were going to use all the computer power to reveal the Investor through his Dark Web connections.

But it turned out the Investor had figured it out straight away by the second theft because he had never done them. He was simply being the fall guy for Eva and Hunter so he wanted to investigate.

Bettie was impressed at his skill. He must have found all the secret emails between Eva and the companies that were going to report their products stolen, when in reality they were going to be safely moved to Eva and Hunter's secret warehouse.

If Bettie and Graham and the happy couple

hadn't of been there, she wasn't sure what would have happened. But one thing was clear, Madeline would have died and Bettie never would have forgiven herself if that had happened.

So she was extremely glad she had been there, and judging by the bank deposit, Madeline was too.

But Bettie had had to call Eva earlier to find out the answer to one very important question that had been bugging her for ages.

How had Eva managed to get the cardboard forensically clean?

At first Bettie had wondered if Eva had been trained in forensic science. She hadn't. Then she wondered if Eva had just bought and researched the necessary equipment. Again she hadn't. It turned out one of the companies that was being blackmailed and that Fisher Insurance insured was a crime scene cleaning company.

So Eva simply made a few phone calls to make sure everyone was protected.

Bettie loved that about other people. No matter how dark the deed (or not in this case) good people still wanted to protect each other, and that was why Bettie was more than pleased when Graham had decided not to charge Eva, Hunter or Madeline with any so-called crimes they had committed.

Because to be honest what crimes had occurred. As far as the lawyers would be concerned, one department of the tech company would have changed the intended destination of the "stolen" computers, and then another department would have accidentally called in a theft.

That's all that happened.

Someone knocked on the door and Bettie smiled as she saw Madeline walk in wearing a long white summer dress with white high-heels and a pearl necklace.

"Thanks for the money," Bettie said with a smile. "Can I do anything else for you?"

Madeline shook her head. "Miss English. Bettie. I just came to tell you the reason why I hired you yesterday,"

Truth be told, Bettie had been wondering that because it would have been too easy for Eva and Hunter to handle things by themselves, and Bettie still couldn't understand why she had to get involved. Considering everything looked as if it was going to be taken care of, without her investigating.

Bettie nodded.

"I hired you," Madeline said, "because I probably knew my husband was alive. Things had been strange at work for ages. I knew something was off with all the companies and policies that Eva and Hunter dealt with,"

"You needed someone you could trust to find what was going on," Bettie said.

Madeline nodded. "Exactly. And because of you, I have. So thank you. Really Bettie, thank you,"

Madeline was about to leave when Bettie gently grabbed her shoulder.

"I have one more question,"

Madeline laughed. "Why did I apparently hit my husband with a spade?"

Bettie nodded.

"Miss English. I truly hope you are never married to a millionaire. He controls you, isolates you and treats you like property,"

Bettie gulped. She was so glad Graham wasn't like that.

"And as you can tell Bettie," Madeline said, "I am not one to be controlled,"

Bettie nodded and stayed silent as she watched Madeline leave. She really hoped that Mr Fisher stayed locked behind bars forever, for no woman should ever be treated like that.

"Bet,"

Bettie heard Graham coming up the stairs to her office and she felt her stomach fill with little butterflies and she was so excited to see him.

"I love you," they both said the second they were at Bettie's door.

Bettie laughed and grabbed her things and they both started to walk down the stairs onto the high street below.

"I'm never leaving you again," Graham said, "you're my crime-solving partner, lover and whatever happens you'll be an amazing mother,"

And as soon as Graham said that Bettie realised how she felt about having twins. She didn't care about that little fact, she was going to be an amazing mother and she was going to give her children the best future they could possibly have.

Especially with a handsome beautiful man by her side, Bettie couldn't wait for the future with Graham by her side. But until then Bettie was definitely going to enjoy whatever plans he had to spoil her with.

Because after being threatened by a so-called madman (the psychologist found out Mr Fisher was lying about the voice), Bettie was going to enjoy her evening.

And she was really, really looking forward to that.

A VERY URGENT MATTER

GET YOUR FREE AND EXCLUSIVE SHORT STORY NOW! LEARN ABOUT NEMESIO'S PAST!

https://www.subscribepage.com/fireheart

Keep up to date with exclusive deals on Connor Whiteley's Books, as well as the latest news about new releases and so much more!

Sign up for the Grab a Book and Chill Monthly newsletter, and you'll get one **FREE** ebook just for signing up: Agents of The Emperor Collection.

Sign Up Now!

https://dl.bookfunnel.com/f4p5xkprbk

About the author:

Connor Whiteley is the author of over 60 books in the sci-fi fantasy, nonfiction psychology and books for writer's genre and he is a Human Branding Speaker and Consultant.

He is a passionate warhammer 40,000 reader, psychology student and author.

Who narrates his own audiobooks and he hosts The Psychology World Podcast.

All whilst studying Psychology at the University of Kent, England.

Also, he was a former Explorer Scout where he gave a speech to the Maltese President in August 2018 and he attended Prince Charles' 70th Birthday Party at Buckingham Palace in May 2018.

Plus, he is a self-confessed coffee lover!

Other books by Connor Whiteley:

Bettie English Private Eye Series
A Very Private Woman
The Russian Case
A Very Urgent Matter
A Case Most Personal
Trains, Scots and Private Eyes
The Federation Protects

The Fireheart Fantasy Series
Heart of Fire
Heart of Lies
Heart of Prophecy
Heart of Bones
Heart of Fate

City of Assassins (Urban Fantasy)
City of Death
City of Marytrs
City of Pleasure
City of Power

Agents of The Emperor
Return of The Ancient Ones
Vigilance
Angels of Fire
Kingmaker

The Garro Series- Fantasy/Sci-fi
GARRO: GALAXY'S END
GARRO: RISE OF THE ORDER
GARRO: END TIMES
GARRO: SHORT STORIES
GARRO: COLLECTION
GARRO: HERESY
GARRO: FAITHLESS
GARRO: DESTROYER OF WORLDS
GARRO: COLLECTIONS BOOK 4-6
GARRO: MISTRESS OF BLOOD
GARRO: BEACON OF HOPE
GARRO: END OF DAYS

Winter Series- Fantasy Trilogy Books
WINTER'S COMING
WINTER'S HUNT
WINTER'S REVENGE
WINTER'S DISSENSION

Miscellaneous:
RETURN
FREEDOM
SALVATION
Reflection of Mount Flame
The Masked One
The Great Deer

OTHER SHORT STORIES BY CONNOR WHITELEY

Blade of The Emperor
Arbiter's Truth
The Bloodied Rose
Asmodia's Wrath
Heart of A Killer
Emissary of Blood
Computation of Battle
Old One's Wrath
Puppets and Masters
Ship of Plague
Interrogation
Edge of Failure
One Way Choice
Acceptable Losses
Balance of Power
Good Idea At The Time
Escape Plan
Escape In The Hesitation
Inspiration In Need
Singing Warriors
Dragon Coins
Dragon Tea
Dragon Rider
Knowledge is Power
Killer of Polluters

A VERY URGENT MATTER

Climate of Death
Sacrifice of the Soul
Heart of The Flesheater
Heart of The Regent
Heart of The Standing
Feline of The Lost
Heart of The Story
The Family Mailing Affair
Defining Criminality
The Martian Affair
A Cheating Affair
The Little Café Affair
Mountain of Death
Prisoner's Fight
Claws of Death
Bitter Air
Honey Hunt
Blade On A Train
City of Fire
Awaiting Death
Poison In The Candy Cane
Christmas Innocence
You Better Watch Out
Christmas Theft
Trouble In Christmas
Smell of The Lake
Problem In A Car

Theft, Past and Team
Embezzler In The Room
A Strange Way To Go
A Horrible Way To Go
Ann Awful Way To Go
An Old Way To Go
A Fishy Way To Go
A Pointy Way To Go
A High Way To Go
A Fiery Way To Go
A Glassy Way To Go
A Chocolatey Way To Go
Kendra Detective Mystery Collection Volume 1
Kendra Detective Mystery Collection Volume 2
Stealing A Chance At Freedom
Glassblowing and Death
Theft of Independence
Cookie Thief
Marble Thief
Book Thief
Art Thief

A VERY URGENT MATTER

<u>All books in 'An Introductory Series':</u>
BIOLOGICAL PSYCHOLOGY 3RD EDITION
COGNITIVE PSYCHOLOGY THIRD EDITION
SOCIAL PSYCHOLOGY- 3RD EDITION
ABNORMAL PSYCHOLOGY 3RD EDITION
PSYCHOLOGY OF RELATIONSHIPS- 3RD EDITION
DEVELOPMENTAL PSYCHOLOGY 3RD EDITION
HEALTH PSYCHOLOGY
RESEARCH IN PSYCHOLOGY
A GUIDE TO MENTAL HEALTH AND TREATMENT AROUND THE WORLD- A GLOBAL LOOK AT DEPRESSION
FORENSIC PSYCHOLOGY
THE FORENSIC PSYCHOLOGY OF THEFT, BURGLARY AND OTHER CRIMES AGAINST PROPERTY
CRIMINAL PROFILING: A FORENSIC PSYCHOLOGY GUIDE TO FBI PROFILING AND GEOGRAPHICAL AND STATISTICAL PROFILING.
CLINICAL PSYCHOLOGY
FORMULATION IN PSYCHOTHERAPY

CONNOR WHITELEY

PERSONALITY PSYCHOLOGY AND INDIVIDUAL DIFFERENCES
CLINICAL PSYCHOLOGY REFLECTIONS VOLUME 1
CLINICAL PSYCHOLOGY REFLECTIONS VOLUME 2
CULT PSYCHOLOGY
Police Psychology

Companion guides:
BIOLOGICAL PSYCHOLOGY 2ND EDITION WORKBOOK
COGNITIVE PSYCHOLOGY 2ND EDITION WORKBOOK
SOCIOCULTURAL PSYCHOLOGY 2ND EDITION WORKBOOK
ABNORMAL PSYCHOLOGY 2ND EDITION WORKBOOK
PSYCHOLOGY OF HUMAN RELATIONSHIPS 2ND EDITION WORKBOOK
HEALTH PSYCHOLOGY WORKBOOK
FORENSIC PSYCHOLOGY WORKBOOK

www.ingramcontent.com/pod-product-compliance
Lightning Source LLC
LaVergne TN
LVHW011846060526
838200LV00054B/4180